E   McPhail, David
     The bear's toothache

7907073

DATE			
JAN 11	Sep22 /09	Jordan	NOV 28
Mar13 202	Nov16 107	NOV 17	FEB 26
May 204	Feb16 109	NOV 24	FEB 27 1992
Oct23 106	Apr13 109		
Dec16 /02	Apr21 128	DEC 15	
Jan22 106	NOV 24	JAN 20	
Feb5 205	APR 22	MAR 3	
Feb13 (22	MAY 03	OCT 13	
Feb27 122	MAR 20	OCT 30	
Mar27 215	OCT 22	NOV 9	
Apr14 108	NOV 22	JAN 23 1999	
Apr23 106	DEC 20	OCT 26	

THE BEAR'S
TOOTHACHE

THE BEAR'S TOOTHACHE

Written and Illustrated by

DAVID McPHAIL

An Atlantic Monthly Press Book
Little, Brown and Company
BOSTON   TORONTO

LIBRARY OF CONGRESS CATALOG CARD NO. 79-140482

Sixth Printing

T 10/72

ATLANTIC-LITTLE, BROWN BOOKS
ARE PUBLISHED BY
LITTLE, BROWN AND COMPANY
IN ASSOCIATION WITH
THE ATLANTIC MONTHLY PRESS

Published simultaneously in Canada
by Little, Brown & Company (Canada) Limited

PRINTED IN THE UNITED STATES OF AMERICA

For my son, Tristian
for Dr. Katherine Leland
for Dr. Arthur Bernstein
and
for Toughie the Bear

THE BEAR'S TOOTHACHE

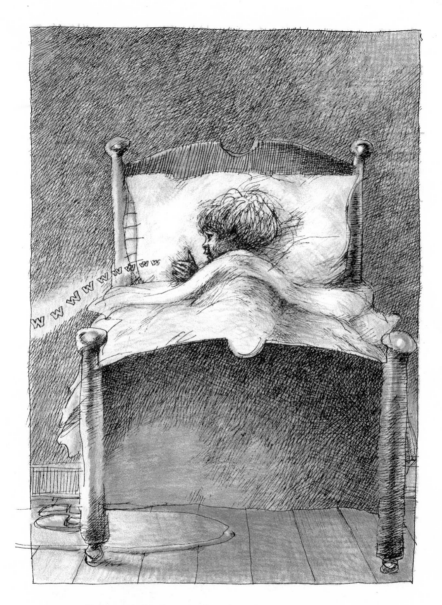

One night I heard something
outside my window.

11

It was a bear

with a toothache.

I invited him in

and examined his teeth.

When I found the one that ached,
I tried to pull it out.

It wouldn't budge.

"Maybe some steak will loosen it
a little," said the bear.
So we went down to the kitchen,
where the bear chewed on some steak
and anything else he could find.

17

Pretty soon the food was all gone,
but the tooth was no looser than before.

When we got back to my room,
I tried to hit the tooth with my pillow.

But the bear ducked,
and I hit the lamp instead
and knocked it to the floor.
Crash!

The noise woke my father,
who got up and came to my room.

24

"What happened to the lamp?" he asked.

"It fell on the floor," I answered.

"Oh," he said, and he went back to bed.

Then I had a good idea.

I tied one end of my cowboy rope
to the bear's tooth

and tied the other end to the bedpost.

Then the bear stood on the windowsill

and jumped.

And just as he hit the ground,

the tooth popped out!

The bear was so happy that
he gave me the tooth

to put under my pillow.